The Hawaiian Christmas Tree

Story by Dawn Adrienne

Illustrations by Susan Brooks

With Aloha
Dawn Adrienne
Susan Brooks
Hawaii

Tamarind

HONOLULU, HAWAII

For Kate and the memory of her at eight years old and for Sarah.

Mahalo Nui Loa to Lei and Jane.

The Hawaiian Christmas Tree by Dawn Adrienne with Illustrations by Susan Brooks
Published by Tamarind, Post Office Box 75442, Honolulu, HI 96836
©1999 Text and illustrations D. M. Casey
Printed in Hong Kong
Library of Congress Catalog Card Number 98-75006. ISBN 0-9667484-1-7

Mama, the Christmas trees are coming to Honolulu for the first time. My teacher says they're coming by ship from Washington about the first week in December. Can we buy a tree, please? It would be so wonderful to have a real Christmas tree to decorate. Please, can we?"

Kalei's mother could see that her eight year old daughter was very excited. "Maybe we can. We will talk to your father when he gets home from work this evening," said Mrs. Keliikoa.

Kalei went outside and sat down under the palm tree. She twirled her long dark hair around her fingers as she thought of having a real Christmas tree this year. Soon it would be December, she was thinking, and the ship would arrive. She felt excited at the thought of decorating the tree.

Kalei liked to make things. She often strung plumerias to make *leis* for herself and her family. Her mother told her that her name meant "wreath of flowers." Now she had to get ready for the Christmas tree that she hoped to buy.

She decided to make a star to put on the top of the tree. She cut the
star out of cardboard and covered it with silver paper she had saved from
chocolate bars. She also strung popcorn to make a garland just the same
way she had strung plumeria *leis*.

Kalei decided she would really like to have a fir tree with roots that she could plant. Each year she would decorate it for Christmas. Later they would put it outside where it would grow and they would keep it for the next Christmas. When she grew up, it would be a big fir tree. Kalei loved Christmas, but she hated that the tree would be tossed aside after the holidays.

"Mama, maybe we will be able to plant the tree and keep it for next Christmas," said Kalei to her mother after talking it over with her father. He agreed it would be fun to have a real Christmas tree for the first time.

"Kalei, the trees are cut but not planted. You cannot expect the tree to live," Mrs. Keliikoa said. Secretly, Kalei felt that it would be possible for the tree to live in Hawaii because she would love it so much—and what about *aloha!* Surely their *aloha* would be felt by the tree. As the tree had not experienced this wonderful feeling before, that would make the difference, she thought. *Aloha* was not available in such abundance in other places as in Hawaii. Kalei was sure her *aloha* would work.

One morning the next week, Kalei was awakened by her good friend,

Alana, whose father worked at the docks. "Kalei, yesterday the *Lurline* arrived with hundreds of Christmas trees. They will be unloading them tomorrow. Isn't it exciting? Are you going to buy one of the trees? I want to, but my mother and father haven't agreed to it yet," said Alana.

Kalei was so excited she would not sit still until her mother and father had agreed to take her to the docks to see the ship with the trees.

They traveled down to the dock area in Honolulu to look at the ship. They were lucky enough to talk to the first mate who told them, "We will be unloading the trees early tomorrow. The merchant who has ordered the trees will then trade them to the individual who will sell them to people such as you, Kalei." Kalei said, "We are going to buy a tree and keep it after Christmas. We will plant it and it will grow." The first mate looked at her mother and father and shook his head. Mrs. Keliikoa shook her head also. They were all doubtful except Kalei who was sure of Hawaii's *aloha*.

Kalei could hardly get to sleep that night. She kept imagining what it would feel like to go and pick out the tree. She said to herself, "We will go first thing in the morning in case the trees sell out quickly. What size will we get— a big tree or a little one? I hope we will know how to take care of it." She drifted off to sleep thinking of Christmas.

The next morning Kalei asked her mother many questions. Her mother was fixing breakfast and finally said, "Kalei, we will just have to wait and ask these questions of the man we buy the tree from. He will surely know the answers to the many questions we have."

Kalei said, "If we share *aloha* and do everything we can to make it feel at home and happy, it will live and we can have it with us always."

"Now Kalei, that is wishful thinking. You know I have explained to you that the trees are cut and cannot possibly live in this climate. We will be lucky if we can keep it alive until Christmas. Please do not get your heart set on having the tree more than a few weeks. When I was a girl we didn't have a Christmas tree but we did have good times in Maui.

My father would go fishing for lobster, and *ulua* and mother would

make a special wine out of sweet potatoes.

Our relatives would visit and we'd have a *lū'au*. We would sing hymns and read stories. We'd eat chicken, *poi* and pig which was cooked in the ground." Her mother had told her many stories of her life on Maui as a young girl. She had moved to Honolulu as a bride with her husband so they could earn their living.

Kalei gathered all the ornaments that would decorate the Christmas tree. Some they had bought at the local variety store and some were the homemade ones. Kalei had seen the *Malihini* Christmas tree across from the Young Hotel so she knew how a Christmas tree should look. The *Malihini* Christmas tree was donated for children in need; gifts were given to the children there every year. She could see in her mind how beautiful her tree would look; she would tie hibiscus and plumeria on the branches if they didn't have enough ornaments. They would decorate the house with *wilelaiki* which had red berries. It would look beautiful.

She went outside to sit in the garden and daydream of how *aloha* would keep the tree green for weeks until they all realized the tree wasn't going to die, but live on with them after all.

Suddenly, a voice broke into Kalei's dreaming. It was her father calling to her to come with them to buy the Christmas tree. Her father drove the electric trolley in Honolulu but today was his day off. He knew how excited Kalei was for Christmas and he wanted to make it as perfect as possible for her.

The moment had finally arrived. Kalei joined her mother and father and they traveled to Kerr's Store at the corner of Alakea and King streets as they had heard that the trees were being sold there. They walked down King until they came to Alakea and sure enough there were many Christmas trees waiting to be sold. The air was filled with the scent of the evergreens. It smelled wonderful to Kalei. She hadn't realized it would be so strong.

Kalei walked around the trees. Her father would hold a tree up, standing it on its trunk and Kalei and her mother would look it over. Some of the trees were beautiful and some had started to droop already. The droopy ones looked unhappy, as if they were sad at having left their home. There were many trees for sale and it took quite a while to look

at them all. Kalei was looking for her tree, a special tree. Which one of these trees was her tree?

It was so hard to choose until she saw a tree that was a little smaller than the others but very healthy looking. It was rather a fat tree. Kalei felt as if this tree was for her. "Mama," said Kalei, "this fat little tree is the one I want. Please let us buy it and take it home."

"But Kalei, there are bigger, taller trees that would be more suitable. Let's look them over again and try to find a bigger one," said her mother. But Kalei wanted the tree she'd chosen and finally her parents gave in and they purchased the fat little tree. They asked the man selling the trees all the questions they had been thinking of: How long would it last? Should they put something in the water in which it would stand? Sugar in the water, he advised; he didn't know how long it would last. He'd heard various times.

They propped the tree up in a deep pail of water as soon as they arrived home. Kalei added the sugar. All the needles on the tree looked green and few had fallen. It looked healthy.

The next day when Kalei went to school, she announced to the class that they had bought their Christmas tree. The children were excited as this was the first time they had heard of anyone having a real Christmas tree at home. Their teacher allowed them to have a discussion about Christmas trees and where the custom of cutting and decorating them had originated. She said, "The first imported tree came in 1903 for the Young Hotel. In 1908, the first *Malihini* Christmas tree was donated by some tourists for Honolulu's children."

Kalei told the class, "My tree will grow and I will plant it in a tub. I will be able to decorate it every Christmas."

Some of her classmates started to laugh and giggle. Tom, the boy who loved joking and making fun of people, said, "It won't grow—it's been cut and will soon die." Kalei felt silly and wished she had not told the class her tree would live even though that's what she believed.

Mrs. Fernandez settled the class down by saying, "It's true the tree had been cut and wouldn't live," but then when she looked over at Kalei she said, "Christmas is the time of high hopes, great joy and miracles."

During recess, Kalei was talking to her classmates and answering their questions. They all wanted to come over to see the tree. Kalei was so happy she said, "Anyone can come over whenever you want to."

After school that day, her father carried in the tree and they put it in a special stand he had made. It had a container for water which they filled before placing the trunk in it. Then after supper came the fun of decorating the tree. The silver star looked very pretty on the top. On went the ornaments including the homemade ones. Kalei's mother had a surprise for her. She had bought some beautiful silver tinsel to drape over the branches. The tree was sparkling!

Over the next week, every day friends and relatives would come to see the tree and exclaim how beautiful it was. The tree actually seemed to be getting greener and the family noticed that very few needles had fallen. They kept the water container filled with sugar water.

As each friend or relative came to the house, the *aloha* was encircling the tree like an invisible tendril.

"*Hūi E Nei. Mele Kalikimaka,*" called Aunt Kolea and Uncle Maka to Kalei and her family. They brought food and they all joined together happy and filled with *aloha* for each other.

They would sit around the tree and look at it, smiling and feeling so happy that they had a real Christmas tree. From time to time someone would go to the tree and express joy at having it and being able to see the loveliness of it. It was truly a gift from heaven, but when Kalei told them she would have it next year, her aunt and uncle looked at Kalei's mother in astonishment. "Kalei dear," said Aunt Kolea, "that cannot be—the tree cannot possibly live." Kalei left the room so she would not have to listen.

Each day some classmates would arrive and ask to see the tree. They said how pretty the tree looked and gently touched the ornaments. The feeling of *aloha* was added with each visit. One day after one of her classmates left, her closest friend, Alana said shyly, "You don't really truly believe the tree will live do you Kalei?"

Kalei looked at her and said, "You are my best friend and you don't believe in my tree, but you are wrong, my tree is going to live because of *aloha*."

As Christmas drew near and the tree had been in their house for over three weeks, Kalei noticed that there weren't any needles on the floor. Her mother had told her as time went on, the needles would fall and the tree would dry up and die. Every day she would go into the front room to look at the fir tree but it was still as green as ever. She gently touched its branches and ran her fingers over the needles even though they were so prickly. She loved the tree dearly.

One day after school, Kalei saw that the star had fallen from the tip top of the tree. She pulled a chair over to stand on so that she could replace

the star. As she reached up to put the star in place she noticed the top was a paler brighter green than the rest of the tree. Then she realized that this was new growth and that was probably the reason the star had fallen. It had been forced to fall as that part of the tree stretched out its new needles. Kalei called out, "Mama, come quickly and see the Christmas tree is growing." Her mother had a difficult time believing this but upon looking closer she recognized the new growth. "What was causing this? The tree is not supposed to grow." Kalei started jumping up and down with excitement.

"The tree is living," she cried out. Her mother said, "There must be some explanation for this—don't get your heart set on it."

Now Kalei, more than ever, believed the tree would live and she spent time with it each day after school admiring it. When her relatives arrived she would show them the tree was growing. They all loved the tree, but didn't believe for a minute the tree would live.

Christmas came along with the presents under the tree. "*Mele Kalikimaka. Hau'oli Makahiki Hou,*" shouted aunties and uncles as they came in the house to celebrate.

The family had a wonderful time opening their gifts, but for Kalei it was the most wonderful Christmas ever because of her tree. Kalei's mother was afraid she was in for a big disappointment when it came time to take the Christmas tree down, but she had to admit to herself the tree looked as green as when they first brought it home.

New Year's was over and the day had arrived to remove the tree. Kalei's father could see by her excitement that she believed the tree was living and he was afraid for Kalei and her disappointment to come. But the time to remove the tree was here.

Kalei began to remove the decorations and pack them away. She chatted the whole time happily. Her father was moving slowly, trying to put off the dreaded moment. Kalei stepped back to look at the tree without the decorations. It really looked very pretty even without them. It looked lovely… and green… and alive.

"Father, we have to get a big pot to plant it in," said Kalei.

"But, Kalei… " he couldn't go on and spoil her wish for a living tree.

She ran out to the shed and found an old pot to plant the tree in. Her father reluctantly helped her carry it into the house. He simply could not bring himself to tell Kalei once again the tree would die. Perhaps they could pretend a little longer. They sat down and talked about Christmas — what a good Christmas it had been. Finally, he could not postpone it any longer so he went to the tree to remove it from the container he had made.

As he reached down to the stump, he was startled and surprised; he exclaimed at once, "Call your mother — this tree has grown some roots." They all peered closer and lo, surrounding the cut trunk were delicate roots several inches long. Mother and father looked at each other.

Kalei said, "We must get it planted in this pot quickly so it will feel at home. Then we can have it with us next Christmas."

And do you know, it lived on for many years.

Hawaiian Words

Aloha:	Love, greeting, compassion, kindness, grace
Hau'oli Makahiki Hou:	Happy New Year
Hūi E Nei:	Hello, beloved
Ka Lei:	The Lei —hence Kalei, meaning wreath of flowers
Lū'au:	Feast
Malihini:	Newcomer, tourist, foreigner
Mele Kalikimaka:	Merry Christmas
Ulua:	Fish (crevalle, jack or pompano)
Wilelaiki:	Christmas berry tree